WRITTEN AND SELF PUBLISHED BY:

ESTD   2024

First edition 2025
Print ISBN 979-8-9935130-0-3
eBook ISBN 979-8218540289

Published by Shelbi Lynn Press

Book cover by S.K. Lynne

CONTENTS

TRIGGER WARNINGS

This is a short work of horror, and while fiction, it contains themes that may be unsettling. Your mental health matters more than any story. Please take care of yourself and step away if you need to.

- Religious trauma & misogyny (severe)

- Graphic violence & body horror (severe)

- Supernatural horror (moderate)

- Death (moderate)

- Pregnancy Loss (mild)

- Sexual shaming (mild)

- Emetophobia / vomiting (mild)

DEDICATION

For those of us still healing from Christian 'Love'.

"Let a woman learn in silence with all submission. I do not permit a woman to teach or to have authority over a man, but to be in silence."
—1 Timothy 2:11–12 (NKJV)

THE FLOCK

"**W**omen should dress modestly, with decency and propriety. In what is appropriate for those who profess to worship God…adorned with good deeds, not vanity. They should learn to fully submit, and never seek to assume authority over men. They must be *quiet.*" Minister Henry's voice boomed from the pulpit and echoed through the small, whitewashed meetinghouse. The wooden pews filled with godly men and women of Ashewell, all nodding their heads in quiet obedience.

It was a typical Sabbath day, spent in the word of God and community. I sat between Esther, my closest friend and the director of our women's knitting circle, and the newest member of our congregation, Lydia. Her family had only recently moved to Ashewell and we instantly bonded over our shared love of gardening (and the secret pots of wild roses we kept hidden behind our homes). The gentleness of her demeanor reminded me of my younger sister, tragically lost to fever two winters ago.

Lydia wore the same plain cotton dress as we all did, but the fabric clung to her in ways that made the modest shift look improper. I caught Esther noticing before the sermon, and we exchanged a knowing look. The curves of her figure drew extra attention. Hell, even I found it hard not to look, the shame of the realization needling up my neck. I knew it wasn't her fault, she was made that way. *Perfect in 'His' image.* Yet it fell to us to guide and teach her the ways of the flock.

Minister Henry continued, "For it was the woman who became the original sinner. Every day, The Enemy works to corrupt and reenter our realm through her." He paused then, letting the words settle like chains around our necks.

I glanced at Esther, noticing how her spine stiffened with each word; her grip tightened on her sacred text so tight I thought the binding might split. She bowed her head in practiced righteousness, lips moving as she recited the words under her breath. She was one of the more educated women in Ashewell. Well studied in the scripture, able to wield verses like a knife. Most would say a natural-born leader. I looked up to her like you would a big sister, always amazed at how easy she made piousness appear.

Sweat began to bead on my back as I bit the inside of my cheek to keep my expression as neutral as possible. This particular sermon had always set my teeth on edge, as I struggled every day, every minute, with my own insubmissive and contrary nature. Each time Minister Henry named a sin, it felt more an accusation than a warning. His gaze crawled over the women, meeting our eyes as if daring us to defy his words.

I told myself to bow my head like the others. Appear repentant. Fit in. Yet I bristled at each command. It was easier for the married women; their husbands' name gave them a sense of safety. I had lost mine in the spring. He'd gone hunting in the woods, and never came back, leaving me without protection or standing within the church. A widow's independence was a dangerous thing here, one wrong word or move, and I could find myself cast out...or worse. I had seen too many women paraded through town and locked in the pillory, shame on display for all to see, and knew what defiance cost.

"For the simple are killed by their turning away, and the complacency of fools destroys them." He continued, voice low as a threat, "I have seen the demons that stalk our town. Waiting for their opportunity to possess. Waiting for us to give in to our sinful nature. We must guard ourselves and each other against greed, lust, envy, pride… and keep them from entering our spirit and possessing our bodies." A whispered murmur of agreement snaked its way through the pews. Sister Sarah's infant let out an ear-piercing shriek, startling many. I wondered if even she picked up on the fear these hellfire and damnation sermons produced.

I yearned to be a good pious woman, but my thoughts were restless. The memories of my mother's bedtime stories brought to the forefront of my mind. I was surrounded by the smell of wood and dust, but I recalled the scent of her herbal remedies and the smoke of her candles. She would whisper tales of the old gods. Of serpents and guardians. Tales the church would deem blasphemy. She could have been cast from Ashewell, yet she still made it a point to teach us that the one and only truth didn't always come from the pulpit.

As the minister thundered on about possession, a sinister thought sunk its fangs into my mind. Is The Enemy really outside of us…or already within? My entire body shivered at the idea, gooseflesh raising the hair on my arms.

"Let us go forth from this sacred space with renewed purpose, carrying the light into the world, and living out the truth we've heard today," Minister Henry finished his sermon, warmth now radiating from his deep voice. "Let us pray."

Brother Daniel's voice rose to lead us in prayer, solid and sure, as the congregation bowed their heads. I couldn't help but to sneak a sideways glance at the people filling the pews, in wonder at their complete acceptance of the ritual.

"…lead us not into temptation, but deliver us from evil." The final prayer concluded with a collective and devout "Amen" from the entire meetinghouse.

My voice cracked as I struggled to get the word out.

The worshippers slowly filed out of the pews, exchanging pleasantries as they passed each other. A cluster of women gathered in the grassy lawn just outside of the wooden meetinghouse, discussing the next knitting meeting and whispering about the latest gossip. They seemed to be drawn to Esther, her voice calm yet laced with holy concern. The ever-perfect pious wife, possessed by her own righteousness. Always the first to name the sin, and last to extend grace.

"Oh Sister Sarah," one woman said, her voice dripping with honey-laced venom "I see you've got a new skirt! It's beautiful but that hemline is so very modern. You know what the scripture says...mode sty is a woman's crown!"

Sarah quickly smoothed her skirt down, trying her best to make it brush her ankles. "Thank you Sister" she responded with a flush on her face.

Another Sister chimed in, one eyebrow raised, mouth pursed, "Widow Eliza, what a bright color of rouge you chose today. It suits you so well. But we all know the scripture says that beauty is fleeting and charm is deceptive. I'm sure He will forgive a little vanity...whatever helps you feel His joy, right?"

Then came the worst of them all. Sister Ruth leaned close to Esther, her voice a murmur but loud enough for those close to overhear, "Poor Sister Hope. We can only pray the loss of her newborn was truly His will...and not His call for repentance."

Sister Hope gasped, as if struck in the chest. Her head bowed, lips pressed into a trembling line. "Yes...His will is good, Sister Ruth."

I listened to the veiled, nasty tone of judgement...the familiar undercutting words of piety. They sweetened their words with scripture, their cruelty sanctified. Claimed demons only entered the *weak*.

I said nothing.

As Esther's husband, Brother Daniel approached, the women moved on to lighter topics.

That's when I saw it. The lustful look he gave Lydia. Not once, but twice. Esther noticed immediately, her eyes burning with jealousy, yet she kept her expression calm. Acted as if nothing was wrong.

Her voice remained steady, but I heard the sharpness. "Mercy, I'll see you for dinner. Ladies, have a blessed Sunday." Her tone turned to ice. "Lydia," her smile too thin to be kind, "next time, line your dress. We are to be modest and avoid temptation, not parade it down the pews. The Enemy only needs the smallest invitation, and it is our duty to keep men from stumbling."

Lydia's eyes dropped to the ground as shame crept up her features. "Yes ma'am." Her shoulders rounded in an attempt to make herself smaller. Everyone said their goodbyes, completely unphased.

As I walked to Esther and Brother Daniel's home, the tension from the group's volatile undercurrent pressed on my mind like stone stacked on a sinner's chest…heavy and unmovable.

That evening Esther served roast lamb and gravy, herbed root vegetables, and warm rye bread. The smell alone made my mouth water upon entering her homestead. I found myself awed by her ability to do everything to perfection. We all sat down at the simple dining table, Esther dishing the meal, making sure Brother Daniel got the best and largest cut of meat. He was blessed beyond measure to have her as a wife.

Serving herself last, Esther took a seat while politely asking him to lead us in grace before a morsel passed our lips.

"Of course darling," his voice carried the undertone of duty one would expect. Typical.

He launched into prayer, "We thank Thee for Thy bounty, O Lord. Bless these provisions to our bodies' nourishment, feed our souls with Thy holy word, and keep watch over Minister Henry, who leads Thy flock with truth and authority. Amen."

Our conversation naturally revolved around today's sermon, discussing scripture and how to best keep our covenant community safe from lurking demons.

Esther spoke, her voice soft, as if this morning's humiliation never happened. "Speaking of today, I saw your eyes linger on Lydia, *dear.*"

Daniel was mid-chew when he huffed a chuckle, "Don't start, woman." I recoiled internally, eyes down to keep my thoughts to myself.

"I wouldn't dream of it. I just wouldn't want it to become a habit," her tone placating to soothe. Whether his ego or her pride, I wasn't sure.

He countered with authority that rivaled Minister Henry, "and what did we learn today? *Women are to be quiet.* Is this how a godly wife would treat her husband?"

"Of course not, my duty is to serve you. You are correct. I won't mention it again," it was small, but I caught how her voice trembled. My heart sank to see my friend shrink in this way. She glanced at me, and for a blink I thought her pupils turned to slits, but I doubted what I saw instantly. Surely not real. A trick of the light.

Daniel finished his meal and got up from the table, leaving his plate exactly where Esther placed it. As we cleaned up she spoke of Lydia again. "I've been praying, Mercy," she said. "It's been put on my heart that Lydia is impure."

Again, I said nothing as my stomach tightened in knots.

"That is not the first time I've caught Daniel looking at her," her voice a hiss. "And where men stumble…it is women who lead them astray." She took my hand, hers cold as ice. "You've seen it too? The way she walks, what she wears. I've read about the Jezebel spirit. How The Enemy cloaks himself in beauty and lust."

My throat went dry. I wanted to say that we should be correcting Brother Daniel, not Lydia. But I nodded in agreement instead.

Esther went on, her practiced righteousness back in place, "I don't feel right allowing this Jezebel to linger in Ashewell. Would you be willing to speak to Sister Ruth? Or we could…quietly mention this revelation at the next knitting circle? To protect the flock, of course." Esther smiled widened, and for the briefest moment I thought her teeth looked…sharper than they had before.

I blinked and it was gone.

My gut told me this was wrong. I knew this would lead to Lydia being undeservingly shunned and cast from the community. I *should* take a stand. But my gut had always opposed the teachings…the gossip and judgment. I told myself to ignore it, fall in line. Be the pious woman. The pressure of denying my friend, of seeming to side with The Enemy, was unbearable.

"Yes of course, Esther. To protect the flock." My voice attempted to replicate Esther's pious tone.

I struggled to get comfortable in my bed that night, constantly shifting back and forth to find some semblance of relaxation. My entire body was exhausted but muscles were tight as a noose. I slept fitfully, and dreamed of Nahashiel. The powerful ancient serpent my mother whispered about before bedtime. She said it was a guardian, the protector of truth. I didn't believe her. The stories the ministers spun always linked the serpent to The Enemy.

The sky was painted in ominous coppers and crimsons, dark like freshly spilled blood. I heard my name carried by the wind, or was it in my mind? I walked barefoot, the gnarly roots of the ancient trees scraping against my feet, realizing the source of my whispered name laid just ahead.

I felt no fear as I approached, despite how enormous Nahashiel was compared to his surroundings. He could easily swallow me whole, nothing but a tiny crumb. He was coiled below a blackened tree like a tower, his scales dull and scarred from age. He watched me with eyes full of knowledge, and I felt his power as I inched closer. I should have been scared, but instead a sense of calm energy enveloped me. His voice came, not from his mouth, *but inside my head.*

You are touched by evil energy. Do you know what you deal with, child?

My brow knit with confusion.

The takeover has begun. Only fire will cleanse.

"Fire? I...I don't understand."

A knitting needle suddenly lay between us, glowing red and swirling with magic.

All ends in ash.

Full of doubt, I reached for the needle anyway. It leapt to my hand, burning hot.

I woke with a gasp, jolting upright, dizzy from the nightmare…a metallic taste filling my mouth. The aroma of mother's herbs and the smoke from her candles hanging thick in the air.

Was that a dream? It felt entirely real. I glanced down to my hand, expecting a blister. There was nothing, just lingering warmth.

I busied myself in the days that followed, throwing myself into the sacred text in a desperate attempt to calm my mind and scrub away the guilt of my insidious thoughts of carrying out Esther's plan. I told myself I was righteous. It's what's best for the flock.

The nightmare was just a silly bedtime story, come back to haunt me. Minister Henry would not lead me astray.

Esther had stopped by on her way to the butcher, red staining her apron, a warm loaf of bread in her arms. Of course, a gift for me. Always on the go, ever the godly wife and friend. She instantly noticed how disheveled I was.

"Mercy! What has a hold of you? I've never seen you in such *disarray*. The circles under your eyes have you looking like a corpse."

I managed to choke out a thin laugh, told her I hadn't been sleeping. Conveniently leaving out that I was possibly losing my grip on reality. She clucked her tongue and set the bread down. "Pray more dear. Scripture is the only balm, and we are doing right by following His word."

Taking a deep breath, I closed my eyes and nodded in feigned submission. "Thank you, Esther."

"You're welcome. Hopefully I won't have to lay eyes on Lydia while in town. If she hasn't lined her dress by now, I'm not sure I can hold my tongue until our next meeting." Bitterness warped her features. Her eyes caught the light for just a moment, the whites seeming to take on a murky green cast.

I did a double take, not trusting my tired mind. Her eyes were normal. It must be the exhaustion. "I'll pray for you. See you then."

Three days had passed, but the dream didn't fade. If anything, it thickened…clotted like coagulating blood. My knitting basket sat untouched near the end of my bed. My frayed nerves kept me from touching it at all. When I finally picked it up, the needles caught the light and shimmered faintly. *Odd.*

The knitting circle met at least once a week, typically a couple of hours before our weekly sermon. I made my way to the meetinghouse, hands sweaty, dread coiling in my gut. My mind was spiraling with obsessive thoughts. Be righteous. Be the good pious woman. Do what's right for the flock. Protect Esther, your best friend.

When I arrived, the scent of wood and dust enveloped me, but was tinged with molder. Sister Ruth and Esther were already in the parlor, needles clinking as they made their loops, the air thick with tension and ruthless judgment.

Lydia still hadn't shown. I desperately hoped she would miss today's meeting, and we could avoid the entire situation. The others filed in and after a short prayer, Esther decided it was time to share her revelation. It didn't surprise me that her timing aligned with Lydia's absence.

"Sisters," she said gently. "The Lord has placed something on my heart, and I feel led to share."

The needles stopped. Silence fell. The women hung on Esther's every word, as if she was the Minister herself.

"It's about Lydia."

The women exchanged glances and put their stitching aside.

"I've seen troubling signs," Esther whispered. "I've prayed for days, and thrown myself into the sacred text. It is obvious she invites lust and tempts our Brothers with her sinful ways. She is a seductress, a Jezebel spirit, infiltrating our flock." She smiled, a bit too wide. Her eyes darkened as they locked on mine.

"Esther..." I started, voice catching. "Should we pray with her first? Before assuming—"

Esther's head tilted as her glare cut through me, silencing the rest. "Mercy?"

My gut wrenched. I knew this wasn't about Lydia. It was about jealousy. Envy. Control.

I gripped my needle so tight my knuckles turned white. My lips parted to object, to tell them all that this was jealousy disguised as piety. Esther's gaze pinned me, her brows raised in a silent command to fall in line. I faltered, the metallic taste filling my mouth. I swallowed the truth, and lied instead.

"Yes. I've seen it too." The lie festered in me, putrid as an open wound left to rot.

Esther nodded. The others murmured in agreement.

Sister Ruth spoke like the judge and jury, her verdict delivered, "Then it's settled. She must be removed."

Not a single one of them thought twice or asked for more proof, and picked up their needles as though we'd merely decided on what color thread to use.

Moments later, the door creaked open with Lydia's arrival. She stepped inside, dressed in a drab gray cloak, carrying her knitting basket along with a fruit pie for the group. "I'm so sorry I'm late! I didn't know what flavor everyone would prefer, so I went with blackberry. I hope that's ok." She looked around the parlor, expecting smiles from the group. None came.

"Lydia," her name crawled from Esther's mouth. "I know what you are, and you are not welcome here."

Lydia blinked, "What? Know what I am?"

Esther's eyes narrowed to slits; her voice laced with evil, not sounding like her own. "Don't play stupid. You are a Jezebel, and your sinful ways will not poison this flock."

Lydia's face turned bright red with shock. "But...I have done *nothing*."

Sister Ruth spoke this time, with her usual sanctified cruelty, "You don't need to. Please leave."

Lydia's eyes darted to mine, begging for me to defend her. I looked down at my knitting instead. The yarn started to blur as tears stung my eyes, but I kept my head down.

She said nothing more, just shook her head in disbelief as she turned to leave. The door slammed with finality.

No one spoke of her and needles continued to clink. The flock felt safer. Their circle knit tighter without the supposed Jezebel in their midst.

The worshippers began to trickle in to the meetinghouse, though the midweek sermon would not start for another hour. It was their time for communing, to catch up with their neighbors on the lawn.

The women were in the kitchen preparing tea and bread. I walked past the side window and froze. There stood Brother Daniel…and Lydia. She giggled at something he said and he moved closer, eyes lingering. Esther appeared beside me before I could move. Her eyes instantly locked on to the scene. She caught the look in Daniel's eyes. Her hands went cold and shook as though she stood in a blizzard.

"Jezebel." She rasped, voice gravelly. "She tempts him *AGAIN.*" Her body began to twitch uncontrollably.

"Esther. Be reasonable." I pleaded. I could feel her rage as it crackled through the air. Her lips whispering scriptures that sounded like blasphemy.

I turned to her just as she snapped. My body locked, terror rooting me to the floor, in shock as I witnessed my friend's face contort in unholy ways.

"He is MINE!" she snarled, the voice that came from her was not her own. Not man nor woman. *Other.*

For a heartbeat the whites of her eyes clouded as if a film had crept across them. Her jaw cracked open, wider than humanly possible, her mouth filling with rows of teeth as sharp as broken glass.

"She is a thief. A whore!" Her words came doubled. The layered voices echoed with fury.

I backed away as her eyes began to rot, the whites began to fill with sickly green mucus that oozed like algae, thick and wet around her lashes. Envy dripped down her face in viscous trails. Her back arched unnaturally as her fingers stretched too long, tendons straining as they ripped into long black claws.

"I WILL TEAR HER OPEN."

Sister Ruth burst into the doorway, sacred text in hand.

"Esther!" she condemned, her voice wavering with fear. "What have you become?!"

Esther tilted her head, sneering as her smile split to reveal her glass shard grin.

Sister Ruth's voice rang out like a bell, "I rebuke you in the name of The Lord. I command all evil spirits to leave this pl—"

Esther lunged, claws sliced through Ruth's neck mid-verse, raking through skin and bone. The sound of ripping flesh louder than her shriek of terror. Blood sprayed across the kitchen walls as Ruth fell to the floor with a thud, her sacred text landing next to her.

Esther stood over Ruth's body, blood dripping from her claws. "Oh Ruth, you should have known that book wouldn't save you. Not from *me*." The rotten mucus hung in strings from her eyes as she stared down at the still warm body, unblinking. Blood pooled under Ruth's corpse, seeping into her sacred text like a mockery.

I wanted to scream, to break down. To run. I backed away slowly, knowing I couldn't continue to sit idly by, couldn't handle being silenced again.

My basket was just inside the pantry door where I'd left it.

Hands shaking, I reached for the knitting needle. It leapt to my hand, pulsing and glowing red, the heat of it nearly burning. A hint of earthy, herbal smoke filled my nose.

"What do you think you're doing, Mercy?" Her voice distorted and inhuman. "You defend *her?* After everything we've been through?"

"You're not Esther," my voice trembled, the metallic taste filling my mouth again.

"You're right about that. Esther opened the gate, and I walked through. Too easy when your flock is ripe with rot. I am *Livyatan,* the demon sent to damn you all to the fiery pits of hell."

She stalked towards me, every step rigid, as if rigor mortis had already set in, claws cutting the air.

I gripped the needle tighter, the heat searing into my palm. I prayed that mother was right about Nahashiel. Hoped that he was more than a fevered dream, and that I carried the strength to do what was necessary.

"Forgive me, Sister," I cried, then lunged before Livyatan struck.

The needle pierced her chest, slicing through fabric, flesh, and bone with the ease of a sword. I continued to push with everything I had, making sure I made it all the way to the heart.

Esther clawed my back to shreds. Pain ripped through me, my fingers slipping on the needle…but I forced it further. The tip hit its mark. Her eyes went wide as her body seized, then collapsed onto the wooden table, igniting like a match. She shrieked as the steel flared, white-hot flames engulfing her cotton dress. Her skin crackled as it blistered and burned. The stench of roasted flesh choked me, acrid as charcoal with a foul, moldering undertone.

For one impossible moment, I saw Esther's eyes again. Clear and furious as she stared back at me. "You will burn *with me*, Mercy." She reached for me, and I stumbled back on to the floor just out of her grasp.

I ran, gathering everyone I could before the fire spread throughout the meetinghouse. We raced through the pews and past the pulpit, everything catching fire as fast as dry kindling. The thought that I killed my friend came faster than the smoke.

I burst out the front doors, collapsing on the lawn. My entire body shuddered violently as bile singed my throat. I heaved the contents of my stomach onto the grass as I watched the divine meetinghouse burn to ash. The fire consumed it all…the demon, the building, the sacred words. The flames burned hotter than they should, scorching the earth so fiercely that even the soil turned black. A permanent reminder. A black mark on hallowed land the flock could never scrub away.

It took time for my wounds to heal, but I eventually made my way back to the ashes. Scarred, yet changed. The blackened earth was rendered unusable, the foundation beyond rebuilding. Wind stirred up fine gray dust, a thin fog that clung to my trousers as I moved slowly through the carcass of the meetinghouse. Nothing remained but the ruins of what we once called holy. Its self-righteous walls had burned away, revealing the hidden rot and corruption they had tried to silence.

I passed the place where the pulpit once stood, remembering how Minister Henry commanded his sermons like a shepherd leading lambs to slaughter. His lectern was gone. Burned to nothing.

I stood where the parlor should have been. Where my greatest shame resided. Where I let Lydia down. The look in her eyes still haunts me. The door was missing, as if the room itself longed to forget that memory.

Near the kitchen, Esther's grin flashed in my mind...not the 'friend' I once looked up to, but the demon with sharp teeth and dripping eyes of envy. I could still smell the sickly-sweet hint of rot that clung to the air.

Then I saw it, shimmering in the light, impossibly untouched by the fire. The knitting needle. I bent and picked it up with trembling fingers. It was still warm, a faint pulse of vibration moving beneath the steel.

I slipped it into my pocket, feeling the warmth, the weight, and the power that remained. No longer a needle, or a symbol of quiet domestication, but a weapon full of ancient energy. I savored the metallic taste that filled my mouth, sharp and undeniable, knowing I held the truth.

Complicity had cost me everything. Silence had cost me my best friend, my faith, my voice, my community.

I would *never* let that happen again.

AUTHOR'S NOTE

The inspiration for *The Flock* came from a mythology short story contest with a few prompts. An earlier, shorter version of this piece was published through that contest, but what you're reading here is the expanded edition.

With everything happening in the US in 2025 (hello, Christian Nationalism), I wanted to write a story that critiqued not only the church, but also the women who perpetuate the patriarchy, while shining a bright light on their internalized misogyny.

Mercy's doubts were intentional. Her instinct that something was wrong was my way of showing how important it is to listen to those feelings and question belief systems. Her mother's bedtime whispers were the voice of every other religion the church silenced, a reminder that truths exist outside the pulpit and deserve the same respect.

I *may* have thrown in one of my own religious injuries with Lydia, and I am sure many can relate.

The demon possession of Esther is an example of how rot can take over inside organized religion. I have not witnessed demons, but I have seen plenty of people weaponize their faith to harm others. That is why I reached for Livyatan, also known as Leviathan, who is often described as a demon of envy. Esther does not simply fall to jealousy and envy, she becomes wholly consumed until she became what she feared the most.

At the same time, I wanted the weapon to be the opposite of monstrous. Something domestic, feminine, ordinary. The knitting needle. The women's circle uses them for quiet submission. In Mercy's hands, it becomes a weapon of truth, fire, and rebellion.

If you're triggered, take a deep breath and ask yourself *why*.

ABOUT THE AUTHOR

SK LYNNE

SK Lynne is an aspiring author, entrepreneur, and book-obsessed dreamer. Follow along on social media (and Amazon) for more stories and general chaos. TikTok & Instagram: @sklynnebooks